Sheltie
Goes to School

Peter Clover

PUFFIN BOOKS

for Robert and Victoria

PUFFIN BOOKS

Published by the Penguin Group
Penguin Books Ltd, 80 Strand, London WC2R 0RL, England
Penguin Putnam Inc., 375 Hudson Street, New York, New York 10014, USA
Penguin Books Australia Ltd, Ringwood, Victoria, Australia
Penguin Books Canada Ltd, 10 Alcorn Avenue, Toronto, Ontario, Canada M4V 3B2
Penguin Books India (P) Ltd, 11 Community Centre, Panchsheel Park, New Delhi – 110 017, India
Penguin Books (NZ) Ltd, Cnr Rosedale and Airborne Roads, Albany, Auckland, New Zealand
Penguin Books (South Africa) (Pty) Ltd, 24 Sturdee Avenue, Rosebank 2196 South Africa

Penguin Books Ltd, Registered Offices: 80 Strand, London WC2R 0RL, England

www.penguin.com

First published 1999
4

Sheltie is a trade mark owned by Working Partners Ltd
Copyright © Working Partners Ltd, 1999
All rights reserved

Created by Working Partners Ltd, London W12 7QY

The moral right of the author has been asserted

Set in 14/22 Palatino

Made and printed in England by Clays Ltd, St Ives plc

British Library Cataloguing in Publication Data
A CIP catalogue record for this book is available from the British Library

ISBN 0-141-30453-7

Chapter One

Emma ran the dandy brush down the
length of Sheltie's back. As she brushed
and brushed, the bristles filled with hairs
and had to be rubbed clean with a comb.
Emma soon had a big ball of Sheltie's hair
in the palm of her hand.

'If I collect much more of this,' she said,
'I'll soon have enough hair to make
another little Shetland pony, just like you!'

Sheltie threw up his head and gave a

loud whinny. It seemed to Emma that Sheltie was laughing.

'You are funny, Sheltie,' Emma smiled. She rolled the loose pony-hair into an even tighter ball and bounced it off Sheltie's head.

The little pony became instantly alert. Two small ears suddenly pricked up between an unruly mop of mane and two bright eyes twinkled with mischief.

The ball of hair lay at Sheltie's feet. The little pony pranced around excitedly, tapping the new-found toy with his hoofs.

Emma scooped up the ball and pretended to throw it for Sheltie to fetch. The little pony ran a quick circle around her and then stood to attention, waiting for a game of catch.

Emma tossed the ball gently towards

him. Sheltie caught it between his teeth just as Emma's mum arrived.

'Yes!' cried Emma as she punched the air. 'You caught it! Well done, boy.'

Sheltie dropped the ball in Mum's hand and blew a soft snort.

Suddenly, Mum had an idea. 'I'll tell you what, Emma. I could make some nice little patchwork ponies for the school fête and use all this spare hair for tiny manes and tails.'

'And make miniature Shelties,' said Emma.

'Exactly,' said Mum, smiling. 'I bet we could sell dozens of them on the handicraft stall.'

Emma thought that was a fantastic idea. The school fête was taking place the following weekend and all the pupils had been asked to bring along bric-a-brac, jumble or handicrafts to sell on the stalls. Emma had already sorted through her old toy cupboard.

'If you make little Shelties, I would probably have enough things to run a stall all on my own,' she said. 'There are all my old dolls *and* their wardrobes, lots of

4

books, my roller skates and heaps of other things I don't play with any more.'

'And I could make some cakes and horseshoe-shaped biscuits to sell too!' said Mum. 'You could call it "Sheltie's Stall".'

Emma liked that idea a lot. 'And we're going to give rides in your little cart as well, aren't we, boy?'

Sheltie answered by tossing his head and blowing a loud raspberry.

'It's going to be the best school fête ever,' said Emma. 'I bet we raise enough money to fix the leaky school roof.'

Sheltie leaned up against Emma and gently pressed his weight against her. The little pony had a terrible itch between his shoulders and he knew that Emma's brush would be just right for the job.

Emma knew exactly what to do. She

rubbed the brush in hard circles and collected enough hair for some more miniature Shelties.

'Looks like you're in for plenty of extra grooming this week, boy!'

Chapter Two

The next morning was Saturday. Sheltie peered at Emma through his shaggy forelock. She was staggering down the garden path, carrying a huge cardboard box which was filled with all her old toys. Sheltie thought they were all for him.

As soon as Emma entered the paddock and plonked the box down on the grass, Sheltie poked his nose inside. Seconds later, he pulled out a rag doll.

'Sheltie, put that down!' But Sheltie took no notice. 'Those toys are for the school fête,' Emma warned. 'And if you make them all wet and soggy, we won't be able to sell any of them!'

Sheltie cocked his head to one side as though he was thinking about what Emma had just said. Then he dropped the doll and Emma popped it back into the box.

Later that morning, Emma harnessed Sheltie to his little cart. She loaded all the unwanted toys and Mum's bric-a-brac jumble into the cart, ready to be delivered to Miss Jenkins at Little Applewood Primary School.

Miss Jenkins had arranged for the school to be open at ten o'clock, Saturday morning. But, according to Mr Grimley, it would close again at twelve o'clock sharp.

Mr Grimley was the new caretaker. Emma didn't like him very much – he was always so grumpy. He lived above the school in the small caretaker's flat. He also had a store-shed, directly opposite his private front door. And if anyone went anywhere near that store-shed, then Mr Grimley would certainly let them know about it.

Emma closed and padlocked the paddock gate while Sheltie pulled his cart out into the lane. The little pony swished his tail impatiently as he stood waiting for Emma.

Sheltie always looked forward to his rides, especially when he had his little cart with him. The cart usually meant that something exciting was going on.

Chapter Three

The little Shetland pony clip-clopped his way along the country lane, pulling his cart behind him. Clouds of dust puffed up from beneath the wheels as Sheltie and Emma set off on their way to school.

Emma hoped that she would run into her best friend, Sally. Sally had a piebald pony, called Minnow, who was Sheltie's best pony friend. Sally had also sorted out lots of things to sell at the fête, and had told Emma that she would be at the school just after ten o'clock.

As Emma and Sheltie approached the school, Emma saw Mr Grimley, the caretaker, sweeping the entrance. He was banging his broom against the wall and muttering under his breath, 'Rubbish, rubbish. It's all I ever do. Sweep up everyone's rubbish.'

Mr Grimley was tall and thin, with a shiny bald head and a big, bushy moustache. He swept a leaf briskly from the playground out into the lane. Mr Grimley didn't like the odd leaf flying around. In fact, he didn't like litter of any kind. And he particularly didn't like the idea of a busy school fête with people messing up his clean playground.

Emma was a bit nervous of Mr Grimley.

And there he was, standing at the school entrance, waiting.

Sheltie, on the other hand, didn't care a jot. He tossed his head and blew a long, fat raspberry at the caretaker. And as if that wasn't enough, the little pony looked him straight in the eye and gave a loud belch.

Mr Grimley eyed Sheltie and his little cart suspiciously. Then he turned to Emma and said, 'I hope you don't think you're bringing *that* thing into my nice, clean playground.'

Emma felt her face turning red.

'He's not a *"thing"*,' she scowled. 'This is Sheltie. And we've brought jumble along for the school fête. It's all been arranged by the teachers. Everyone's bringing stuff this morning.'

'Yes, I know!' muttered the caretaker. 'Nothing but trouble, these school fêtes. Just make sure you don't spill any of that jumble in my clean playground! And keep away from my store-shed,' he added.

Emma could feel Mr Grimley's eyes boring into the back of her head as she led Sheltie across the spotless school yard.

The cheeky pony tossed his mane at the caretaker as he trotted his cart over to the smiling teacher.

'Oh, what a nice cartload of goodies,' said Miss Jenkins. 'We'd better get this lot safely inside straight away.'

Sheltie stepped forward immediately, ready to pull his little cart right into the school classroom.

'No, Sheltie!' cried Emma. 'We've got to unload all the jumble first. Stay out here and behave while we carry everything inside. And try to keep out of Mr Grimley's way,' she whispered.

Emma and Miss Jenkins carried everything inside. A spare classroom was being used to sort through and store everything until the day of the fête.

All the desks had been pushed together into rows and were already piled high with old toys, books, ornaments, bric-a-brac and assorted jumble. Half of it had already been labelled and priced.

'Some of the children came really early,' said the teacher. 'But they didn't stay very long. They all left their boxes and things with Mr Grimley and then just went home again.'

Emma glanced out of the window at the new caretaker. She hoped Sheltie was behaving and keeping well out of his way.

Chapter Four

Emma finished helping Miss Jenkins in the classroom and then went outside to find Sheltie.

She'd told the little pony to stay by the door and keep out of mischief. But when Emma stepped outside into the school yard, Sheltie was nowhere to be seen.

'Sheltie! Sheltie!' called Emma urgently. She hoped Mr Grimley wouldn't hear her. The last thing Emma wanted was the grumpy caretaker coming to check up on her.

Suddenly, Emma heard a familiar sound. It was Sheltie whinnying to her from across the playground. The little pony was over on the other side of the yard, standing right next to Mr Grimley's precious store-shed.

'Oh, no!' cried Emma. She looked around anxiously for the caretaker, but luckily there was no sign of him. Emma hurried across the playground. Sheltie was pawing at the shed door with his hoof. The words 'Keep Away' were painted on the door in big red letters.

'No, Sheltie! Stop that at once!' Emma called.

Sheltie turned his head and flicked his long forelock out of his eyes. There was

something very interesting in Mr
Grimley's store-shed and Sheltie wanted
to let Emma know about it.

He pranced on the spot and danced his
hoofs on the grey tarmac as Emma took
hold of his reins.

The little pony blew a series of loud
snorts and pushed his muzzle up against
the shed's small, dark window. His breath

steamed up the glass pane as he tried to peer inside.

'Come away, Sheltie,' urged Emma. She tugged at the reins, but Sheltie wouldn't budge.

Emma glanced over her shoulder. When she saw that the coast was clear, she was tempted to take a quick peek through the window herself.

It was very dark inside the shed and Emma couldn't see a thing. But she could *hear* something. And so could Sheltie. His ears twitched as he listened to the strange rustling sound coming from inside.

'There's someone in there!' whispered Emma.

Sheltie looked at her as if to say 'I told you so,' then snorted and shook his head from side to side.

Emma pressed one ear against the wooden door and listened hard. Sheltie was so excited, he kept blowing soft whickers in Emma's other ear.

'Not now!' whispered Emma. 'I can't hear a thing with you doing that.' She pushed Sheltie away and listened again. Yes! There was definitely someone in

there. Emma was quite sure that she heard a small voice cry out.

'And just what do you think you're doing?' someone barked suddenly. It was Mr Grimley. He stood in front of them with his hands on his hips. The caretaker's moustache bristled angrily as he wagged his finger at Sheltie.

'And what's that *thing* still doing here?' he barked. 'I've told you before. Keep away from my store-shed!' Mr Grimley sounded really angry. 'Now get that animal out of my clean playground. You know the rules. No pets inside! No animals outside! And no mess!'

Emma didn't have to be told twice. She turned around and, taking large strides, she led Sheltie away from the shed as fast as she could.

Sheltie blew a rude snort and rumbled his cartwheel over the nasty man's foot.

'Ow!' yelled Mr Grimley. 'You did that on purpose!'

Emma didn't stop or look back. She led Sheltie across the playground with the little cart bumping along behind them.

They reached the school gate just as Sally rode up on Minnow. Sally had two carrier bags of jumble tied to her saddle.

'What's the hurry, Emma?' said Sally.

Sheltie blew a cheeky snort and rubbed noses with his friend Minnow.

'Grumpy Grimley caught us looking through his shed window,' said Emma.

Sally pulled a face and laughed. 'You mean you actually went near enough to look in through the window?'

Emma grinned and nodded. 'It was

24

Sheltie's idea,' she said. 'He went right up
to the shed and I had to go and fetch him.'

'But Grumpy Grimley yells at people if
they go within ten metres of it,' said Sally.
'He's even painted "Keep Away" on the
door.'

'I know,' said Emma. 'And now I know
why!'

'Why?' asked Sally eagerly.

'Because he's got someone locked up in there,' exclaimed Emma. 'That's why!'

Sally gasped. 'Are you sure?'

'Positive,' said Emma, beaming. 'Just before Grumpy Grimley came and yelled at us, I heard a voice inside calling for help!'

Chapter Five

'If you're certain you heard something, then we should tell someone straight away,' urged Sally.

Emma suddenly looked doubtful.

'Well, I *thought* I heard someone,' she said. 'But I'd want to be absolutely certain before I told anyone.'

'Oh, no!' groaned Sally. She had a sudden feeling that she was about to be roped into one of Emma and Sheltie's adventures. 'And I suppose you're already thinking up a plan, aren't you?'

Emma just stood there and grinned. Sheltie wiggled his nose and huffed a soft snort.

'Just dump that jumble and I'll tell you all about it,' said Emma.

Sally left her bags just inside the school gate and set off with Emma and Sheltie, back up the lane.

As they rode along, Emma told Sally the first part of her plan.

'We'll never get anywhere near that shed on a school day,' she began. 'Grumpy Grimley always stands guard next to it at playtime.'

'And after school he sweeps and does odd jobs outside,' interrupted Sally. 'I've seen him when I've been out riding.'

'So that just leaves tomorrow,'

announced Emma. 'Sundays are always quiet in Little Applewood. And I was thinking, maybe Mr Grimley goes out on Sundays.' Emma raised her eyebrows as she spoke. 'If we spy on him,' said Emma, 'and he goes out, then you and Minnow could follow him while Sheltie and I investigate the shed.'

'Why can't you and Sheltie be the ones to follow him?' questioned Sally. 'I don't like the idea of spying on Mr Grimley. He might start yelling if he sees me.'

'No, he won't,' said Emma. 'But he might if he saw Sheltie and me. Then he'd probably forget to go wherever he's going and follow us all the way back down the lane to make sure we're not going anywhere near his playground or his precious store-shed.'

Sheltie snorted noisily and bobbed his head up and down. It was almost as if he were telling Sally that Emma was right.

'Besides,' added Emma, 'I'll be spying too! I'll be hiding with Sheltie and waiting to see if Mr Grimley leaves his flat. But we'll only know if he goes anywhere if you're there to follow him!'

As they reached Sheltie's paddock, Sally gave in. 'Oh, all right, Emma!' she huffed. 'You win.'

Emma smiled up at her best friend and poked her playfully in the ribs. 'I knew you'd want to help. Now, as soon as I get Sheltie out of his harness, I'll saddle up and race you to Horseshoe Pond. I bet you can't wait to hear the *second* part of my plan!'

*

Sheltie and Minnow were loosely tethered as Emma and Sally sat beneath the big sycamore tree at Horseshoe Pond. It was the perfect spot for talking and making plans.

'I'll bring a torch,' said Emma, 'and some paper and a pencil.'

Sally looked puzzled, but listened carefully.

'Then we can shine the torch through the window and see if there's anyone locked inside,' explained Emma.

'And what's the pencil and paper for?' asked Sally.

'That's the clever part,' said Emma with a grin. 'If Mr Grimley *has* got someone locked up in there, we'll push the pencil and paper under the door and get them to write a message. Then we'll have *proof* that there's a prisoner trapped in the store-shed.'

Sally had to admit it was a brilliant idea.

'Foolproof,' said Emma, beaming at her friend.

Chapter Six

The next morning, Emma got up early and
fed Sheltie his breakfast. The little pony
seemed extra frisky today. As soon as he
saw Emma running down the garden
towards his paddock, Sheltie galloped a
quick circle, then rolled on to his back and
kicked all his legs in the air.

'You are funny,' said Emma, laughing.
Sheltie always made her smile and feel
happy. She suddenly thought about Mr

Grimley. She had never, ever seen *him*
smile. Or laugh! He always looked so
grumpy and sad. It can't be very nice
being like Mr Grimley, thought Emma. She
wondered why he was so miserable all the
time.

When Sheltie had finished his pony mix,

Emma gave his thick coat a quick brush and combed out his long mane. She cleaned off the brush with a comb and collected another ball of Sheltie hair for her mother's patchwork ponies. Then she looked at her watch. It was almost time to saddle up and meet Sally.

They trotted slowly down the lane, past all the cottages. Then Emma took Sheltie round to The Crescent – a small alleyway that ran behind the village and joined the road leading out from Little Applewood. It was a short cut and came out at the other end of the High Street, just a little way along from the school. Sally and Minnow were already there, across the road, waiting.

Sally was standing next to her pony, pretending to adjust her stirrup leathers.

She glanced across at Emma and nodded by way of a signal.

Emma and Sheltie stopped at the end of The Crescent and hid behind a big, bushy tree that grew there. Emma wanted to hide so that she could spy on the caretaker's flat without being seen. If Mr Grimley sees us, he'll get suspicious, thought Emma.

But Sheltie was in no mood for standing still. He thought this bush looked very tasty. The little pony reached up and pulled at some of the leaves. This made the whole bush shake.

'No, Sheltie!' warned Emma. But the leaves were too green and fresh for the little pony to ignore. Sheltie pulled another mouthful and the bush trembled again.

'Stop it!' whispered Emma.

Then she looked up and saw Mr Grimley coming out of his flat. The caretaker was dressed in his best Sunday clothes and was walking briskly towards the school gate.

If Sheltie shook the bush again, then Mr Grimley was bound to notice. Emma quickly leant forward, across Sheltie's neck and reached out with her arm to scratch his chin. This usually made Sheltie

stand still and close his eyes. If she stretched, she could almost reach the little pony's chin. Mr Grimley was about to walk past at any moment. Emma stretched a little further.

Sheltie closed one eye but kept the other one open to look at the juicy, green leaves.

Emma stretched even further and scratched. Then she felt herself slipping from the saddle.

'Oh, no,' she gasped.

Thump! Emma landed noisily on the grass.

'Good morning, Mr Grimley,' boomed a loud voice from nowhere. It was Mrs Price, the headmaster's wife. 'Lovely day for a brisk walk,' she said. Then she linked her arm through his and dragged him along at a fast pace.

'I'm on my way to the bus stop,' said Mr Grimley. 'I always visit Emily on Sundays.' And then they were gone.

'Phew!' breathed Emma. 'That was close!' She peeped through the leaves and saw Sally and Minnow following close behind.

Sheltie gave a loud belch, then lunged his head back into the bush for another mouthful of leaves.

When Emma was sure that the coast was clear, she edged Sheltie out into the road, climbed back into the saddle and quickly trotted across to the school.

They waited there for Sally and Minnow to return.

Sure enough, just a few moments later Sally and Minnow came hurrying back up the road at a fast trot. Minnow's hoofs clattered noisily on the hard road and made a terrible din. Sheltie added to the noise by snorting a loud welcome to his best friend.

'Well, if the rest of the village was asleep,' said Emma with a smile, 'they'll be wide awake now!'

Sally was breathless with excitement. All she managed to say was, 'I saw him. He got on a bus. I saw him. Grumpy Grimley's gone for a bus ride.'

'So far, so good,' said Emma, grinning.

Chapter Seven

Emma unhooked the wooden gate and quickly rode Sheltie into the school playground. Sally followed on Minnow, but kept looking back over her shoulder – Sally wasn't as daring as Emma. She kept thinking that someone might be watching them and that any minute, they'd be in big trouble.

'No wonder he's always keeping a close watch on that shed in case anyone gets too near,' said Emma. 'He'll be in big trouble if there *is* someone locked up in there.'

But Sally didn't answer. She was too busy staring at the shed window.

'Look, Emma!' cried Sally. 'Someone's stuck newspaper up behind the glass.'

'Not *someone*!' exclaimed Emma. 'Mr Grimley! And what he's done proves

there's someone in there, doesn't it?'

'How?' asked Sally.

'Well, he would only put paper up,' said Emma, 'if he didn't want anyone to look inside!'

'Or didn't want whoever's inside to look out!'

As Sally spoke, Sheltie pushed his muzzle against the window and tried to lick the paper through the glass.

'Look at Sheltie,' said Emma. 'He's trying to tear the paper down.'

Suddenly Emma looked puzzled.

'What is it?' asked Sally.

'I don't get it,' said Emma. 'Whoever's locked inside could easily take down the paper – unless, of course, they've been tied up!' She rapped loudly on the door with her knuckles.

'Hello!' called Emma. 'Is anyone in there?' No one answered. Even when Sheltie snorted loudly through the keyhole, there was no reply.

'They must be gagged too,' said Emma.

'Tied up *and* gagged!' repeated Sally. 'That's horrible. We *must* tell someone!'

'But we still have no proof,' sighed Emma. Then her face brightened a little. 'I'll try the notepaper under the door!'

Sally watched Emma push the pen and paper carefully under the shed door. Emma left a little bit of the paper sticking out so that she could pull it back out again if necessary.

'It won't be any good if they're tied up and gagged,' said Sally.

Sheltie stared down at the corner of white paper poking out from under the door. Then he carefully placed the tip of his hoof on it and pulled it out.

'No, Sheltie. Leave it alone,' said Emma. She pushed the paper under the door again. 'We've got to try, Sally,' continued Emma. 'After all, we *do* need some evidence before we can tell anyone.'

While she was talking, Sheltie pulled the paper out again with his hoof.

'Sheltie, I told you, NO!' said Emma. This time she sounded quite cross and ended up pushing the paper back too hard. They all watched as it disappeared completely under the shed door with a whoosh!

'Now look what you've made me do, Sheltie,' said Emma.

Sally was about to laugh when the piece of paper came whooshing back out, followed by the pen.

Emma couldn't believe it. The paper
was blank. She pushed the paper and pen
under again. And once more, out they
came.

Emma banged on the door. 'We were
only trying to help,' she yelled, still

hoping there might be an answer. 'Do you want to stay locked in there for ever?'

But still there was no reply. Nothing. Suddenly, Sheltie pricked up his ears and they all heard a strange rustling sound coming from behind the door. Then it stopped as suddenly as it started.

'I don't like this,' said Sally. She looked really worried.

'Neither do I,' agreed Emma. 'But at least we now know there is definitely someone in there! We both heard it, didn't we?'

'Maybe it's just Mr Grimley playing a game,' said Sally. 'Perhaps it's his way of scaring us, to keep people away.'

'But it can't be the caretaker in there,' said Emma. 'I saw him leave his flat and you saw him get on the bus.'

'Well,' said Sally, 'whoever is locked inside that shed obviously doesn't want to be rescued.'

Emma couldn't understand it, but she had to agree.

Sheltie blew a loud snort and sniffed at the gap under the door. He seemed very puzzled too!

Chapter Eight

For the rest of the afternoon, all Emma could think about was Mr Grimley's store-shed. She didn't talk to anyone about what she had been up to in case she was told to keep away. Mum certainly didn't like Emma snooping around other people's property. But Emma hoped that even her mum would understand if she knew the full story.

Anyway, Mum was busy making little

patchwork ponies for the school fête. And Dad was having a snooze with Emma's toddler brother, Joshua, on the sofa, so Emma didn't like to disturb them.

Emma quickly popped her head round the door of Mum's workroom.

'I'm just taking Sheltie out for a late afternoon ride,' said Emma.

Mum looked up from her sewing machine and smiled. 'Don't be too long though,' she said. 'We'll be having tea at five.' Then she took up a piece of material and began stitching another pony.

Emma strolled out to the tack room to fetch Sheltie's saddle and bridle. Sheltie saw her immediately and came galloping across to the fence.

'Fancy a ride, boy?' called Emma as she swung his bridle across her shoulder.

Sheltie tossed his head and gave his answer by neighing loudly.

Then, as Emma went to lock the tack-room door, she suddenly noticed how big the key was.

She remembered one day last summer, when Dad had mislaid the key to his tool shed, he had used Sheltie's tack-room key to open the door. Dad had had to wiggle

51

the key a bit in the lock, but in the end, it had unlocked the door.

Emma thought she would give it a quick try herself. Just to see if *she* could make the big key unlock Dad's tool shed.

Carefully, Emma pushed the key into the lock. The keyhole was big and worn. The key felt stiff at first, but as Emma wiggled it from side to side she felt it

move slightly. Then *click*! The key turned and the door swung open.

'Yes!' Emma gasped with wonder. If this key could open two locks, she thought, then maybe it could open three.

Sheltie called impatiently from the paddock with a loud whinny. He was wondering why Emma was taking so long.

'All right, I'm coming,' shouted Emma. She quickly slipped the key into her pocket and went to saddle him up.

'Guess where we're going, Sheltie?' said Emma, grinning, as she tightened the girth strap.

The little pony blinked at her and pricked up his ears. He didn't understand what she was saying, but Emma guessed that somehow Sheltie knew.

They took the short cut behind the village. Then they raced past the school and doubled back behind the grass playing field.

Emma was careful to keep out of sight and tried to ride Sheltie behind walls and hedges as much as she could. They dashed between bushes and hid behind trees, hoping that if Mr Grimley was back, he wouldn't see them. Finally, they managed to creep up behind the low stone wall that separated the playing field from the main playground.

Sheltie stood with his chin resting on top of the wall and looked across to the caretaker's shed. Emma looked too. First at the shed, then at the window of Mr Grimley's flat.

'How can I try the key without being

seen?' whispered Emma. Suddenly her idea seemed very foolish.

Sheltie blew softly through his lips and stared at the window too. Then Emma noticed that the curtains had been pulled across.

'That's odd,' she said. Emma looked at her watch. 'It's only half past four. But it's lucky for us,' she added. 'That means Mr Grimley is inside, but he won't be able to see me.'

Sheltie made a grunting sound and nibbled on a dandelion he found growing in the wall.

Emma left Sheltie to enjoy his snack and hopped over into the playground. She hoped that the curtains would stay drawn and that Sheltie would keep quiet and out of sight on the other side of the wall.

She turned to face Sheltie and pressed a finger to her lips. 'Shhhh!'

The little pony let out the softest whicker and blinked his eyes sleepily.

Emma tiptoed up to the shed and pulled the key from her pocket. She quickly glanced across at Mr Grimley's window, then slipped the key gently into the big lock.

Chapter Nine

Emma's hand was shaking as she turned the key. But nothing happened. She tried again.

This time she pulled the key out slightly. The key felt stiff in the lock. Emma wiggled it and suddenly the key turned with a loud *clunk*.

'Yes!' breathed Emma. 'It works.' She turned to Sheltie who was peering at her from over the wall, then at Mr Grimley's drawn curtains. Finally she looked back at the shed door and reached for the handle.

Emma's heart was beating fast as she turned the handle and pulled the door open wide. But what she saw inside gave her quite a surprise. There was no prisoner to rescue. No one tied up and gagged. There was nothing. Nothing at all. Mr Grimley's store-shed was completely empty!

Emma quickly closed and locked the door, then tried to pull out the key. But it was stuck fast. Emma pulled hard and tried again. The key wouldn't budge.

'Oh, no!' said Emma, panicking. 'Please don't be stuck.'

At that moment, Sheltie blew a really loud snort. Emma thought she saw Mr Grimley's curtains twitch and her stomach turned a double somersault. She gave the key one last tug and pulled it clean out of the keyhole. Phew! Then she dropped it with a clatter on the tarmac.

At any minute Emma expected to hear Mr Grimley yelling at the top of his voice. But there was no sign of him.

Emma tucked the key safely back into her pocket and ran over to Sheltie. She dived over the wall and pulled the little pony's head down next to hers. Sheltie thought this was a new game and blew in Emma's ears.

'Stop it,' whispered Emma. 'I can't hear a thing.'

They listened carefully for the sound of footsteps. Hearing none, Emma dared to look over the wall.

Sheltie looked too and peered into the

school playground from beneath his bushy forelock.

Nothing had changed. Mr Grimley's curtains were still pulled across and there was no sign of the caretaker anywhere.

'Come on, Sheltie,' said Emma. 'Let's get out of here!' Suddenly Emma wanted to be as far away from that spooky store-shed as she could get.

The next day at school, Emma told Sally everything that had happened.

'An empty shed!' exclaimed Sally. 'Nothing inside at all?'

'Nothing,' said Emma.

'Then why does he try to keep everyone away from it all the time?' asked Sally.

'I don't know,' said Emma. 'But I *do* know one thing. That shed gives me the creeps!'

Chapter Ten

As the week passed, Emma tried to forget all about Mr Grimley's rotten old shed. Everyone at school was looking forward to the fête on Saturday. And at home, Emma was busy helping Mum finish off the miniature Shelties she was making.

Emma's job was to make manes and tails for the little patchwork ponies and to glue them on. There were twenty-five ponies altogether.

Miss Jenkins had decided to create a special stall where only pony things would be sold. Mum's miniature Shetlands would go on sale next to framed pony pictures, pony ornaments, pony-print table mats, colouring books, T-shirts, pony cushions, magazines, models and much more. There was also a 'pin the tail on the pony' game, a pony lucky dip and Mum's horseshoe biscuits. And of course, Sheltie would be giving rides in his little cart.

On Friday afternoon there were no lessons in the classroom. Instead, everyone helped to set out the stalls for the school fête the following day. Emma's mum and some other parents came along for a little while to help the teachers. Mum had brought Sheltie along with her. His little cart was very useful for carrying things.

Outside in the playground, helpers were rushing to and fro setting out wooden tables.

Bunting and coloured flags were strung out from stall to stall – soon it didn't look like a school playground at all. And all the time, Mr Grimley stood outside his shed with his arms folded across his chest, watching.

'I hope he's going to be in a better mood tomorrow,' said Mum, just before she left. 'Otherwise he's really going to spoil things!'

At four o'clock, when all the preparations were finished and everyone was setting off home, the headmaster sent Mr Grimley into the village to buy some raffle-ticket books from the Post Office.

Emma and Sheltie found themselves
alone in the playground.

As soon as the caretaker had
disappeared through the gate, Sheltie was
off, dragging the cart across the
playground.

'Come back!' yelled Emma as she
chased after him.

Sheltie's ears were pricked and alert as he trotted towards Mr Grimley's shed. Sheltie had heard something.

Oh, no. Not again, thought Emma.

She tried to pull Sheltie away. 'Mr Grimley will be back any minute!' she pleaded. But the little pony just wouldn't budge. He stood firm outside the shed and snorted loudly.

Then Emma heard something too. There was no mistake this time. From inside the shed a woman's voice called out loud and clear.

'Help me! Help me! Help me!' Over and over again, the voice cried and cried.

Emma didn't know what to do. She tried the door handle, but the door was locked.

'Who's in there?' called Emma. 'Can

you hear me?' But there was no answer. The voice had stopped.

'Hello? Hello?' called Emma, but again there was no reply. Sheltie whickered softly and made low whimpering noises against the window.

'If you're just playing games,' said Emma, 'then you should stop it!' She sounded quite cross. 'Whoever you are, it's not funny!'

Sheltie shook out his mane and blew a raspberry for whoever was inside.

'Come on, boy,' said Emma. 'Let's go home. It's just someone being silly.'

She jumped into the cart and urged Sheltie forward. 'Walk on, boy.'

The little pony trotted away across the playground and headed for the open gate. Emma couldn't resist taking one last look

over her shoulder. But seconds later, she
wished she hadn't. The newspaper across
the window had been torn, and a funny-
looking eye was blinking and staring out
at her through a small hole.

Emma gasped, then flicked Sheltie's
reins. They quickly trotted the rest of the
way home with Emma bucking and
bumping along behind in the little cart.

Chapter Eleven

On Saturday morning, Emma helped
Mum carry all the patchwork ponies she
had made out to Sheltie's little cart.

Sheltie was full of beans this morning
and pulled the soft toys out of the cart as
quickly as Emma could pile them in.
Sheltie liked the smell of these little
stuffed ponies. He sniffed at their hairy
manes and tails, then blew a puzzled
snort.

'I don't think Sheltie understands why these little toy ponies smell just like him,' said Mum, laughing.

Emma took a bright blue one from a carrier bag and held it up for Sheltie to look at.

'That's *your* hair, Sheltie,' explained Emma.

Sheltie took a big sniff, then sneezed hard and blew the pony clean out of Emma's hand.

Then Sheltie quickly lowered his head and gently picked up the soft toy in his mouth. He handed it back to Emma with a muffled snort.

'I hope you're going to be this good at the fête,' said Emma, smiling.

Sheltie's eyes twinkled with a look of mischief that Emma knew usually meant trouble.

When Emma and Sheltie arrived at school, the playground was already busy with helpers. People were filling the stalls from big cardboard boxes – one was already full of homemade toffee apples, sweets and biscuits. Another was brimming with pots and jars of jam and country pickles. There were stands selling toys, some selling books, and others selling clothes, bric-a-brac and jumble.

Sheltie's pony stall looked great. Miss Jenkins had found some tea towels with different kinds of ponies printed on the front, and had hung them up at the back of the stand. There were pony posters, pony jigsaw puzzles, pony books and magazines, pony ornaments and lots of other pony things neatly arranged around the stall.

'Look at that, Sheltie!' grinned Emma, pointing to a wooden board next to the stall. It was a special painted notice which said: 'Once around the playground with Sheltie the Shetland Pony, 50p a ride'.

'That's your job, Emma,' said Miss Jenkins. 'I'm sure everyone will want a ride in Sheltie's little cart.'

She handed Emma a tin can on a string for collecting the money.

ONCE AROUND
THE
PLAYGROUND
WITH SHELTIE
THE
SHETLAND
PONY

50p A RIDE

Sheltie cocked his head to one side and
looked at the notice. Then he pranced on
the spot, ready to go.

'I think Sheltie's looking forward to
giving these rides,' said the teacher,
smiling. 'Let's get these patchwork ponies

out on display, then you'll be ready for your first customer.'

Luckily it didn't take long. The playground was already filling up. People were busy rushing around buying things from stalls and playing the side-show games. Within just a couple of minutes someone asked, 'Can I have a ride, please,' and dropped fifty pence into Emma's tin. It was Sally.

Emma laughed. 'You don't have to pay, silly. You can have a free ride any time.'

'But I wish to take a tour of the grounds in your carriage immediately,' joked Sally in a posh voice.

'Oh! Certainly, madam,' answered Emma, trying hard not to giggle.

Emma led Sheltie, and trotted him once around the playground with Sally waving to everyone like a queen from her royal carriage. As they passed each stall, people looked up and waved back.

As usual, Mr Grimley was standing in front of his shed with both arms folded across his chest.

Sally waved as she passed. And for a brief moment, Mr Grimley smiled.

'Look at him guarding his empty shed,' said Sally.

Emma had been trying to forget all about the strange staring eye she'd seen and the voice calling for help. She hadn't even told Sally. She told her now.

'An eye!' exclaimed Sally. 'Are you *sure*?'

'Positive,' said Emma. 'A small, black, beady eye.' It made her shiver just thinking about it. 'It was staring. Staring at

Sheltie and me through a hole in the newspaper.'

'Then there *is* someone in there after all,' said Sally.

'Definitely,' said Emma.

Just then, someone else came by for a ride and Emma and Sheltie had to go.

This time, as Sheltie passed the caretaker's shed his ears pricked up and he blew a loud snort. And for the rest of the morning, every time Sheltie gave a ride and pulled his cart past the shed, his ears went up and he snorted loudly.

'It's that shed,' said Emma. 'Sheltie knows there's something in there.'

'I think we should tell someone,' said Sally.

'I know,' agreed Emma. 'But what if they force Mr Grimley to open the door and there's no one inside again? We'll look like silly, nosy troublemakers.'

Just then, Emma's neighbour, Mr Crock, ambled past. He was carrying an enormous birdcage that was almost as big as himself.

'Good morning, you two. Morning, Sheltie,' he said brightly. 'I've brought this along for the fête. It's been cluttering up my shed for years.'

Sheltie sniffed at Mr Crock's waistcoat and nudged him playfully in the side. This made Mr Crock stop walking and put down the cage. Then Sheltie stomped his hoof hard on the ground and blew a long whinnying snort.

'What's the matter with Sheltie, Emma?' asked the old man. 'He seems upset about something. Does he want me to have a ride?' Mr Crock climbed into the cart and settled himself down.

Emma knew she could trust Mr Crock. She was just about to tell him all about Mr Grimley's shed when the caretaker himself walked past carrying a huge box of heavy books for Mrs Price, the headmaster's wife.

'If you could just put them in the boot of the car,' boomed her loud voice, as she hurried ahead, 'I would be very grateful.'

Then, before Emma could do or say anything to stop him, Sheltie was off. The little pony trotted boldly along, bumping Mr Crock across the playground in the little cart.

'Where are we going, Sheltie?' said Mr Crock, laughing, as Sheltie made his way through the crowds.

People heard the sound of the trap and jumped out of the way.

Sheltie zig-zagged in between the stalls without crashing into anyone or knocking one single thing over.

'Yahoo!' yelled Mr Crock.

Emma and Sally dashed after the pony-powered rocket. Emma knew exactly where Sheltie was heading and wasn't

surprised when he stopped right outside Mr Grimley's shed.

A group of parents began to gather round Sheltie and a teacher started taking photographs of Mr Crock in his chariot. Sheltie was posing and snorting excitedly.

But suddenly, all the fun and laughter stopped as Mr Grimley yelled, 'Get away from my shed. Can't any of you read? It says keep away!'

A terrible silence descended like a dark rain cloud.

'There's no need to be so rude,' said a woman, raising her eyebrows. 'There's been no harm done.'

And then, as though Sheltie had been waiting for an opportunity, he nudged the door firmly with his nose and gave a loud whinny.

'Stop that pony!' yelled Mr Grimley. 'Stop him doing that.' But Sheltie wouldn't stop. Again he nudged at the door and whinnied loudly.

Finally, the caretaker grabbed a handful of Sheltie's mane and tried to pull him away.

Emma was furious. She jumped forward and yelled, 'Leave Sheltie alone! He's only trying to help whoever's locked inside.'

'Locked inside?' repeated the teacher with the camera.

'Yes. Locked inside,' said Emma. And she began telling everyone about the strange sounds they had heard coming out of Mr Grimley's shed.

When she had finished, Emma noticed that the caretaker's face had turned a sickly white.

'That's nonsense,' said Mr Grimley
shakily. 'There's nothing in there except
tools.' His voice suddenly sounded
different. Softer.

'Then why don't you just open the door
and let us see for ourselves,' said Miss
Jenkins.

Suddenly, Mr Grimley looked very
worried.

'I can't,' he lied. 'I've lost the key.'

The key. Emma thought quickly. She felt in her pocket. Yes, Sheltie's tack-room key was still there. She had forgotten to put it back on its special hook.

Emma waved the key in front of everyone's surprised faces.

'This key can open that shed,' she announced.

Then, before anyone could stop her, Emma thrust the key into the lock and gave it a hard turn.

'Please be careful!' Mr Grimley cried out in alarm. His voice didn't sound angry any more. It was kinder and filled with concern.

The lock went *clunk* and Emma pulled the door open.

Then she screamed.

Something bright green, with dark beady eyes and flapping wings flew out of the shed and soared over her head.

Sheltie tossed his mane and blew a sharp snort as the parrot circled the shed twice, then landed on his head.

'A parrot!' cried Emma. She shot a glance at Sally who was standing with her mouth open, staring.

Suddenly, the two girls felt a little silly. A *parrot*!

The parrot seemed quite happy and settled down in a nest of hairy mane.

'Help! Call the police,' it cried. 'Save me, save me. A nice cup of tea. Hello, darling!' Once the parrot saw that it had a captive audience, it wouldn't stop squawking.

Mr Grimley stepped forward, held out his arm, and lifted the parrot on to his shoulder.

'I think I've got some explaining to do,' he said quietly. 'But first let me introduce you to Mrs Finnigan.'

The parrot spread her wings and whistled loudly on hearing her name.

'Cor! Who's a cheeky Charlie,' she squawked.

Sheltie cocked his head to one side and seemed to listen along with everyone else as the caretaker told his story.

'Before my dear wife, Emily, was taken into the nursing home,' he began sadly, 'she was sick for many years. Mrs Finnigan was her companion and sat on a perch in her bedroom. Mrs Grimley taught her to talk and chatter. They even watched TV together. And Mrs Finnigan picked up lots of sayings and learned to mimic voices.'

'She sounds just like a real person, doesn't she?' said Emma.

Mr Grimley smiled. 'Yes,' he said. 'And not only does she *sound* like a person,' he continued, 'but she *acts* like one too. She was always playing tricks and games on Mrs Grimley. And it gave Emily something to look forward to every day.'

'Then why do you keep her locked away in that shed?' asked one parent.

The caretaker looked down at his shoes. He seemed really embarrassed.

'After my wife became so ill that I couldn't look after her at home,' Mr Grimley continued, 'I took this job at the school to pay for the nursing home and moved here to Little Applewood. But unfortunately, pets are not allowed in the caretaker's flat, so I had to think of a way to keep Mrs Finnigan with me.

'I couldn't get rid of her,' the caretaker went on. 'She means so much to Mrs Grimley. The shed seemed the ideal solution. I thought that if I kept everyone away, no one would discover my secret. And every night I could sneak Mrs Finnigan back into the flat.'

'Oh dear,' said Mrs Price. 'It's all a bit of a mess, isn't it? But I think the "no pets" rule only applies to cats and dogs. I'm sure the headmaster would allow you to keep a little parrot in the flat!'

'Especially when it's so special to Mrs Grimley,' said Emma. Suddenly she felt really rotten about misjudging the caretaker. Now that she knew the truth, Emma wanted to make it up to him.

'Well, that's why I was always worried about people fussing around the shed,' said Mr Grimley. 'I was afraid that someone would discover my secret. And I can't lose Mrs Finnigan. I'm planning to take her with me next Sunday, on visiting day.'

Sheltie shuffled forward and pressed his nose into the caretaker's arm. Mrs Finnigan looked down and squawked, 'Hello, darling!'

Everyone laughed. Everyone that is,

except Mr Grimley. The poor man looked so worried.

'Chin up,' boomed Mrs Price. 'I'll have a word with my husband. I'll tell him you've simply got to keep Mrs Finnigan in the flat and that's all there is to it!'

Emma grinned. She somehow knew that Mrs Price always got her own way. Even if it meant bending the rules a little.

'And there's this huge bird cage,' said Mr Crock. 'It would be perfect for your Mrs Parrot. And you can have it free! A present from Little Applewood.'

Sheltie shook out his mane and made Mrs Finnigan ruffle her feathers.

Emma laughed. And Mr Grimley even managed a smile, which to Emma and Sheltie made it all worthwhile.

In fact, Mr Grimley looked different

when he smiled. And it suddenly made Emma realize how wrong she had been. Underneath his grumpy exterior, Mr Grimley was rather nice. After all, he was only trying to protect Mrs Finnigan. And all the time he was worried about losing his job and not being able to look after his wife in the nursing home.

Emma decided that from now on, she was going to be extra nice to the caretaker.

Sheltie whickered gently and nudged Emma with his nose. He seemed to be thinking the same thing too!

The school fête turned out to be a big success and raised enough money to fix the leaky roof. Mr Price, the headmaster, was very pleased. He let Mr Grimley keep Mrs Finnigan in the caretaker's flat and even allowed the parrot to visit the classroom on special occasions to 'talk' to the pupils.

'Having a pony as nosy as Sheltie can even turn a school fête into an adventure,' said Sally, as the two girls set off on their way home.

'Having a pony like Sheltie turns *every* day into an adventure!' said Emma with an enormous grin.

If you like making friends, fun, excitement and adventure, then you'll love

The little pony with the big heart!

Sheltie is the lovable little Shetland pony with a big personality. He is cheeky, full of fun and has a heart of gold. His owner, Emma, knew that she and Sheltie would be best friends as soon as she saw him. She could tell that he thought so too by the way his brown eyes twinkled beneath his big, bushy mane. When Emma, her mum and dad and little brother, Joshua, first moved to Little Applewood, she thought that she might not like living there. But life is never dull with Sheltie around. He is full of mischief and he and Emma have lots of exciting adventures together.

Share Sheltie and Emma's adventures in:

SHELTIE THE SHETLAND PONY
SHELTIE SAVES THE DAY
SHELTIE AND THE RUNAWAY
SHELTIE FINDS A FRIEND
SHELTIE TO THE RESCUE
SHELTIE IN DANGER